The Power of Childhood Dreams

TO HELP YOU HAVE A SUCCESSFUL FUTURE

Linda Hehir
and
Louise Blair

ISBN: 978-1-968970-63-5 (sc)
ISBN: 978-1-968970-64-2 (e)

Rev. date: 09/17/2025

The Power of Childhood Dreams is a fictional story. However, the elements used in the story of the "Law of Attraction can" be verified. All the characters' names, (except for Liam my grandson) are the product of the authors' imagination, and any resemblance to actual persons, living or dead is purely coincidental.

We the authors, would like to thank Liam (son and grandchild respectively) and Jaquie Walker and her daughters for proofreading the book and for their helpful suggestions. We would also like to thank Mark Andrews (PeiPei) of Fiverr.com for the images included within this book.

CHAPTER 1

The Old Man and Liam

'Mum, Mum, come quick! An old man has tripped and fell on the river path. His head is bleeding and he is not getting up' Liam breathlessly shouted as he ran home to fetch his mum.

They both hurried out to the path where the old man was sitting holding his head. Liam and his mum helped the gentleman to his feet and invited him to their house so they could clean his head wound and cover it.

'I don't want to be any trouble madam' he muttered 'I shall just rest on the seat by the river until I feel a bit better'.

'Don't talk nonsense! I am glad to be able to help. It's not too far to the house. Oh and my name is Cath,' said Liam's Mum.

'Please come. We can call a doctor' offered Liam 'I think

you must have been unconscious for ages! My name is Liam, by the way' Liam said holding out his hand to the old man to shake.

'Very pleased to meet you, my name is Mr Tom Kerr', accepting Liam's hand shake with his free hand. The old man agreed to go to the house, but refused to be seen by a doctor.

'My mum used to be a nurse', said Liam. 'She will be able to clean up and dress your wound no problem.'

"Here let me help you" Cath offered. Cath took Mr Kerr's arm, while he rested his other hand on Liam's shoulder. Helping him, they all walked slowly to Liam's home.

CHAPTER 2

John

Later that afternoon, Liam and his friends, John and Mary were sitting in their gang hut at the bottom of John's garden. The hut had an entrance from the garden itself and exit onto the path by the river.

It was a warm autumn day and they had left the doors open to keep the hut cool.

Liam, John, and Mary were all 10 years old and had known each other since starting school.

Mary was always asking questions. 'What do you guys dream of being when you are older?' was her first question today.

'I'm going to be famous' John said quickly, lying back on his bean bag with his hands behind his head.

Mary knew this would be true as John was really fun, everyone loved being around him and he came up with some awesome ideas.

Building the hut was actually John's idea! Liam being the most convincing of the three and the planning expert, made it happen by convincing John's mum and dad into letting them build it.

'What will you be famous for?' giggled Mary.

John smiled brightly and said 'I will be a great singer, of course'.

Mary laughed, singing wasn't quite what she had expected him to say.

'Let's hear you sing then'.

'I can't just sing like that Mary, I need music to sing along with'.

'Okay John I'll play something for you on my Ipod and you can sing along'.

'Yeah, that will be great. I didn't know you could sing?' said Liam questioningly.

Looking around shyly John replied 'I'm not singing here, somebody might hear me and I'm not good yet'.

'Well this is a good time to practice; it will be like the X factor and Mary and I will be the judges. Oh go on John, it will be fun and we won't laugh or anything' promised Liam.

Mary turned on her iPod and chose Katy Perry - Hot and Cold, 'sing along to this one'.

John looking red in the face and shaking his head, shouted 'NO WAY!!! That's a girls song. 'Can you play something by Michael Jackson?'

Mary found the song Smooth Criminal, and as it played John started to mumble some words in a very low voice.

'Sing louder' both Mary and Liam said 'we can't hear you'.

John feeling silly wished he had never said anything about wanting to be a singer. Laughingly he said 'okay I can't really sing. I just know that's what I want to do when I'm older. Hey!' he continued 'what about you two, what do you want to do when you're older?'

CHAPTER 3

Liam and Mary

John looked at Liam and then Mary and back at Liam questioningly. Liam said 'I want to be rich and live in a big house and have a flashy car and a swimming pool and travel the world'.

'How are you going to do that then?' asked John.

'I don't know yet!' exclaimed Liam. 'But I dream about designing or inventing a solar powered device for generating electricity that's smaller than the panels on our roofs. They are so huge and ugly'.

Mary looking surprised said 'WOW, that's amazing'. John piped up saying 'No way! That's a crazy idea.

By the time you are old enough to invent something they won't be being used anymore. Something else will be being used. Anyway you don't know how to invent something like that'.

'Yeah- you're right John. I don't know how to do it yet, but I will learn what I need to know, and it's no more crazier than your idea. How about you Mary what do you want to be'.

'Me? Emm? I haven't made up my mind yet. I think my dad wants me to become a doctor like him, but I don't know. He seems to work all the time and doesn't have anytime to spend with my mum and me. When he does come home he is so tired and tetchy" explained Mary. 'I think I would like to become rich too but not have to work such long hours, so I can have fun with my mum'.

CHAPTER 4

The Old Man's Dreams

It was beginning to get dark outside and Liam was getting hungry. He was just about to say it was time for him to go home when they all heard a branch breaking outside the hut and then a cough. Startled and feeling scared by this they all turned to look at the exit door onto the path.

'Who's that' John asked Mary and Liam in a quivering hushed tone. Mary and Liam shrugged. Liam slowly and quietly crawled over the door to peek out onto the path.

Suddenly a body filled the doorway. Liam let out a squeal and fell back into the hut.

'Hello there, don't be scared I'm not going to harm you' said the man as he knelt down outside the door and looked kindly at the three children within. 'Allow me to introduce myself, my name is Tom and I am very pleased to meet you all.

I was sitting by the river and overhead what you were talking about and just wanted to come over and say hi'.

Recognising the old man, Liam was the first to recover from the shock and said 'Hey guys it's OK, I know who he is', Liam told the others.

Turning to Tom, he said, 'Hello again. I'm Liam, remember from this morning. These are my friends Mary and John.'

'We were just leaving to go home. We're not allowed to talk to strangers but I guess your not a real stranger as I helped my mum take you up to our house. You do remember me, don't you?'

'Yes Liam I remember and I wanted to thank you for fetching your mum when I fell. It was very kind of you and your mum to help me.

Your mum is a warm and generous lady and I was grateful for the help. I'm sure she wouldn't mind me talking to you for a few minutes if that's ok with you?

I overheard you talking from my seat by the river path and I just wanted to tell you a secret about getting rich and realising your dreams. You see dreams can be powerful if you want them bad enough'.

To Liam, Mary and John, Mr Kerr seemed ancient. he had white hair and a white beard and lots of wrinkles on his face. He was dressed in jeans and a warm jumper, which seemed too big for him.

Liam stared at Mr Kerr's eyes, thinking they were the colour of cornblue flowers. In the growing darkness, his eyes seemed to sparkle like the stars in the sky.

John and Mary were still unsure whether they could talk to the man. Standing up to leave they suggested to Liam that they go home now.

'Wait a minute guys. I want to hear what he has to say. He's the old man I told you about earlier who fell on the river path. My mum and I helped him.'

Look he's very very old and we can escape quickly into the garden if he moves from where he is' said Liam to his friends.

Turning to Mr Kerr, Liam sat on one of the logs in the hut and asked 'So.. how do you know about getting rich? Are you rich then?

CHAPTER 5
Getting Rich

As the man smiled at Liam, Mary and John sat down again. Mary didn't feel so scared now, in fact she felt a warmth spreading over her when she saw the man smile. However, she could feel John trembling at her side and reached out to take his hand.

Then, when the old man began to speak, John, still holding Mary's hand, started to relax and became mesmerized by the sound of the man's voice. It was a deep, low voice but sounded musical.

'Many years ago when I was your age, I also had a dream that I would become rich. Both my parents were very poor, we hardly had enough food to keep us alive and our house wasn't much better than this hut you call your gang hut.

I used to dream and dream of having lots of money until my dad died of a disease'.

'What's a disease?' asked John.

Mary turning round to John said 'don't be silly, everyone knows a disease is something you have when you are very ill'.

'Oh! Well, I didn't know that' said John, 'and anyway, my father isn't a doctor like yours. Liam did you know what a disease was?'

Nodding his head Liam said 'Yeah I knew that'

John thought Liam was fibbing as he would have said more if he really had known.

The old man continuing with his story explained 'if my father had the disease today he would still be living but in those days, there was no medicine available to make him better.

It was then that my dream changed to becoming a doctor so I could stop other people from dying.

I didn't know then how I could do this; I didn't go to school and I couldn't read and write. But I just knew that some day I would be a doctor and I kept telling myself this over and over again.

One day not long after my father's death I went to the

well to fetch some water for my mother; we didn't have running water in those days just the village well.

At the well I met a man who had stopped there to rest from his journey. He asked me my name and where Bloomingdale House was. I told him the house was nearby and I could show him the way if he wanted. He accepted my offer and ...'

John interrupted saying 'What's this to do with getting rich then?'

'Haha! Give me time John I'm not as young as you and I have to tell the story of how it happened in my own way, so you will understand.

Anyway, it turned out this man was the new doctor for our village. While walking with him to Bloomingdale House, I told him that I wanted to be a doctor but I could neither read nor write.

I thought he would laugh at this, but he didn't. Instead, he invited me to come to his house everyday for one hour and he would teach me how to read and write.

"Why would you want to do that?" I asked.

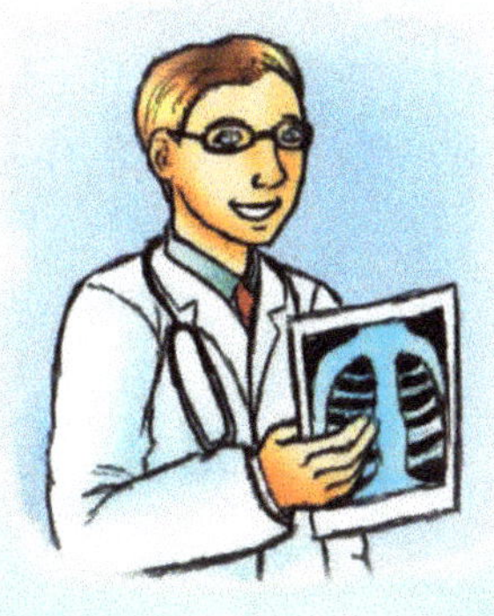

He said many years ago someone helped him to realise his dream of becoming a doctor and as he had no family he wanted to help me to achieve my dream, but only if I was certain that was what I wanted.

"Oh yes, yes," I said "I want to help people get well so other daddies and mummies don't need to die and leave their children". He seemed satisfied with that and we agreed I would visit him every morning at 7am to start learning, but he insisted I must study hard even when I wasn't with him.

Over the following years, he taught me to read and write, about mathematics and the sciences and about life in different towns and countries.

He also taught me some things about anatomy and physiology and medicine. Sometimes he even let me help him do things in his clinic.

I studied hard and did as much work as I could around the house for my mum and around the doctor's house, to help repay him for what he was doing for me'.

'You must have been very clever to learn all that' stated Mary. 'I don't think I could have done that. I don't really get very good marks at school'.

'Ah Mary; all that we are is the result of what we think. You can do anything you choose to do Mary, you only have to believe it. I am no more clever than you are Mary but I really, really wanted to achieve my dream.

At night I would see myself as a doctor in a big hospital and would feel great joy and thank god that I was a doctor. And joy of joy when I was 15, Dr. Graham, paid for me to go to college, and then paid for me to go to university.

'That's so cool, he must have been a rich man' said Liam.

'Can you imagine how happy and grateful I was to this man. I felt rich beyond my wildest dreams that I was receiving everything I needed to become a doctor. The college work was difficult but I was determined to succeed.

The day I finally graduated from university as a doctor, I cried with happiness, just as much as my mother did. She kept hugging me and telling me how proud she was of me and how proud my dad would have been.

Not only did I profusely thank Mr Graham and my mother who encouraged and supported me over the years, but I also remembered to thank god as well and still do'.

Interrupting Mary announced 'I don't think I believe in god'.

'That's ok Mary, I didn't either especially when my father died, but over the years I have come to believe. Anyway I loved being a doctor, it was hard work and long hours but the satisfaction I received from it was so great I did not mind the hard work.

However, when I was about 35 years old I began to feel something was missing. Thinking about what I was missing, I realised I wanted romance, marriage and a family. You see being rich isn't just about having money. It's also about giving and receiving love from loved ones, spending time with them and being passionate about whatever career path you choose. A fulfilled life is what makes a person truly happy.

That night lying in bed I remembered how I became a doctor and started to dream and visualize that I had met a girl I could love, marry and have a family with. My dreams made me feel happy and I thanked god that I was happily married everyday.

A few months later when working in the hospital I met a nurse, who I instantly knew was the woman I wanted to be my wife. Within a year I was married to the most beautiful woman and we had two wonderful children.

Sadly my wife died of old age 2 years ago, however, my children are living in Australia and Canada, both are successful doctors.

'You must be lonely being on your own' said John 'I wouldn't like that'.

Since my wife died I have been traveling to many countries and meeting lots of people and children like yourselves, so that has helped me not to feel so sad and lonely.

I chose a life of helping people and I always want to tell the people I meet about my life, in the hope that they too can find great joy and happiness and riches like I did from using what I now know to be called The Universal Law of Attraction'

'Whats that?' Mary and Liam asked in unison.

CHAPTER 6

Law of Attraction

'Well' said Tom 'it's about attracting what you think or wish for. The universe is made up of energy and our bodies are made up of energy and every time you think of something you want or wish for with real feeling, joy, happiness, sadness or anger your thoughts will be transmitted to the universe.

Some people call this sending a message to their god, like me, or to their angel or even just to the universe itself. Just like when you send an email or text message to someone.

All the really rich people in the world know about this Law and have become rich because they use the Law to help them get what they want'.

'Hey, wouldn't it be great texting your own angel to tell them what we want' Liam said. John and Mary laughed at this nodding their heads in agreement.

'You see the universe will respond to your wish and give you what you need to know or to do for your wish to become true. You just have to be able to recognise it when it comes along.

The message from the universe can come in many

different ways. For example in a dream, in a person turning up that can help you, in something you read or listen to.

In my case, it was easy to recognise when Dr. Graham came into my life. Beware though because if you send a wish out to the universe feeling anger, or hurt or pain you will get back more anger, hurt and pain.

It's important that you always feel joy and happiness about what you want and hold the image of it in your head while thanking god or the universe for it until you have received it and even after you have received it.

Always remember to thank the universe or god every morning for all the good things you already have. This could be things like how good it is that you can see, hear, walk, have parents, this hut, your friends. The list is endless'.

'So?' asked Liam 'It's when you really, really want something and you can imagine what it would be like to have it and you feel all happy and stuff and be thankful in a way as if you already have it and then a message is sent to the universe?'

'That's right Liam, well done. If you can remember this as you are growing up you will achieve the things you want. You may change what you want at anytime as you learn more and more at school.

Always remember to use the same process over and over again. Things might not happen right away but keep your belief in it and something will happen that will show you the way.

Also, you must keep learning about the thing you want to do to become rich, as without some action on your part it may not be possible for the universe to give you your wish.

In my case, I was indeed very fortunate with Doctor Graham coming into my life but I had to put in the time and effort to learn.

Well then, I must be on my way. It's dark now and your parents will be wondering where you are. Bye now and thanks for listening to me and I wish you to become the best you can be in whatever you do'

CHAPTER 7

Being Thankful

After saying goodbye to Tom the children asked each other if they believed his story. None of them were sure if they did or not, but all agreed it would be great if it was true.

'You know something' said Liam as they were all leaving the hut to go home. 'Tom looks kinda like my grandpa'.

As Liam strolled home he remembered helping his grandpa plant a tree in his garden and his grandpa telling him it was called a wishing tree. Maybe my grandpa also believed in the Law of Attraction he thought.

Later that night all three children just before they went to sleep thanked god or the universe for all they had by saying I am so happy and grateful that I am healthy and have good parents and so on.

John added a thank you for being a singer and started humming a few bars of a tune.

Liam added an extra thank you for having ideas and for all the money he was going to receive to buy a big house, for his mum and for him to travel lots.

Mary's extra thank you was for her dad spending more time with her mum and her.

A few days later when she returned home from school Mary was taken by surprise, because her dad was sitting at the dining table with her mum. She ran to him and gave him a big hug and cried with joy.

Her dad sat her on his knee, kissed her head, told her he loved her and said sorry that he hadn't been around much and that he was going to spend more time with her and her mum.

Mary didn't want to leave his knee but she had arranged to meet the boys at their gang hut and she was desperate to tell them how well her positive thoughts and saying thank you had worked.

When Mary entered the gang hut, only John was waiting with a great big grin on his face, he told her how he had been practicing his singing while walking down the street and people kept stopping to compliment him. John could tell that Mary was bursting with excitement to tell him her story too, 'what about you Mary?' he asked.

Mary with a big smile on her face began by explaining how she loved her dad very much and missed him because he was always working and she didn't see him much. 'Mum always tells me how hard dad works to make sure they have nice things for a good life and so they could go on holidays. But you see John I would rather have dad home more'.

'Any way over the past few nights I wrote a letter in my journal saying how glad I am for the time I have with mum and dad together as a family and thanked god for it as the old man told us to.

I'm so excited because today I got my wish when dad told me he was taking us on holiday and would spend more time with us from now on'. Jumping up with joy and laughing she said 'it's so great I just can't believe I've got my wish and so quickly.

I wish I had known about the Law of Attraction sooner. What do you think John?'

'I'm so happy for you Mary. Maybe there is something in the old man's story after all' said John.

Mary and John had been in the tree house for around half an hour and there was still no sign of Liam. Mary asked John 'do you know where Liam is? What can he be doing? We always meet at the same time so he couldn't have forgotten. Lets go round to his house and find out what's going on'.

CHAPTER 8

Liam's Inventions

They both left to go to Liam's house, John humming as they walked over the lawn. When they got there, Liam's mother told them Liam has been up in his room all day, only coming out for a sandwich and random household items. She agreed that Mary and John were welcome to go up and see what was going on since she had been asked that his bedroom was a strictly !!NO PARENTS ALLOWED ZONE!! for today anyway.

Liam was always collecting random things that he found when they were in the woods or down by the river - funny looking stones, wire coat hangers, strange shaped sticks, plastic bottles, etc. They didn't really think he actually kept them until they entered his room.

There on his desk and on his shelves were all the things he had made out of all of the items he had collected. There was one of the plastic bottles he had collected made into what looked like a rocket sitting on its side attached to a tech deck skateboard.

Liam explained that by using just vinegar and baking soda. He could make the rocket take off along the desk. The wheels on the tech deck skateboard made it travel further than it would on its own.

There was also two wire coat hangers attached together and decorated with treasures collected on Liam's adventures with John and Mary. 'That's my adventure station' said Liam very proudly. 'I made it last night to remind me of all the places we have been and time we have spent together, as your friendship is one of the things that I am very thankful for.'

John and Mary could see he was working on a new project. On his table was a small digital clock, 2 potatoes, 2 nails, copper wires, and some alligator clips.

Liam told them he was going to make the potatoes into a battery to get the clock to work. He put one of the copper wires into one side of the potato and in the other side, he inserted a nail. He did the same to the other potato.

'To make it work you have to connect the alligator clip to the copper wire on one potato and connect the other end to the positive side of the battery port in the small clock, then you take the clip to the nail on the second potato and connect it up to the negative side of the clock's battery port. Watch this' Liam exclaimed as he connected his last alligator clip to the unused copper wire on potato one to the unused nail on the second potato.

To Mary and John's complete amazement the clock turned on!!

'Wow' said Mary.

'That's a great trick' shouted John.

'It's not a trick' Liam told them, 'Its Science!! To become an inventor, you first have to know how things work.'

Liam told them how over the past few nights he had decided to try out the old man's methods for getting rich and famous. He explained how he had said all the things he was thankful for, to the universe.

He was thankful that he had great family and friends and that one day he would be known just like Alexander Graham Bell who invented the telephone or James Watt who invented the steam engine.

Liam also enthusiastically mentioned how in the morning when he was going to the shop for his mum he saw a poster in the window advertising a science fair.

'The winner would get his name in this year's Best Inventions Magazine' said Liam. With a beaming smile, he added 'It will be the first step in letting people know my name and what I am capable of'.

Liam had been practicing different ideas all morning for showing at the science fair. 'The science fair is the following week' he explained 'and you have to be able to show the judges how my invention was made, so I will have to keep it simple'.

Liam's younger sister was crazy about Fairies, her whole room was covered in fairy posters and ornaments and bedding so he had decided to make something just for her, but he was going to keep it as a surprise'.

CHAPTER 9

Science Fair

The week running up to the science fair Liam, Mary and John all focused on their dreams.

John's mum had agreed to get him piano lessons to help him with his music and Mary spent amazing evenings playing board games and watching old films with her family.

They still met at the gang hut every day to share their progress and plan what they were going to do next. They were so alive with excitement and in their mind, they could see Liam being awarded a prize for his invention.

On the Saturday Morning of the Science Fair, Liam was up at 5am as he was too excited to sleep any later. It felt like Christmas morning. He hadn't let anyone see what he had been doing and his mum seemed even more excited than he was.

His mum had made his favourite breakfast - pancakes, bacon and Maple syrup, just like they had on holiday earlier in the year. Enjoying his breakfast helped to calm his nerves and he felt energised after it. He wore his lucky shirt (the blue one) and he even put on some of his dad's aftershave so the judges would think he was very grown-up for a boy of his age.

Liam's mum, dad, and sister set off as a family for the Fair in his mum's Mazda. He felt like fairies were jumping up and down in his tummy. Although excited, Liam began to feel a bit afraid until he remembered what the old man had told them in the hut.

With this thought, he began to see himself on the stage at the fair and this made him feel happy and thankful especially as he could see that he had won the prize for his age group at the science fair.

Mary and John and their families were already there when Liam arrived, all desperate to see what he had made. Liam set off for his station telling his friends and family to wait until he was ready.

Liam had asked the fair organisers earlier for a dark corner so that he could show his invention properly. When he had set everything up, he finally invited his family to come and see what he had been doing.

He had a large cardboard box, with one side cut out of it, over the top of his invention so you could see in! He had created a solar powered fairy light just for his sister. It was glowing and looked just like little fairies all in a jar.

The children all turned to see Liam's mum when they heard her gasp. His mum had tears in her eyes as she beamed with pride at her son.

After about an hour waiting backstage at the fair, it was finally Liam's turn to be interviewed by the judges after they had examined his invention.

The judges were very impressed and asked Liam to explain how he had come up with the idea.

He explained about his sister's fascination with fairies and how he wanted to do something nice for her birthday.

Liam explained how he started with a large empty jam jar and dabbed glow in the dark paint into the inside using a paintbrush, explaining that it's better to use different colours and do lots of small dots close together, rather than large dots further apart.

'You should then leave the jar out in the sunlight for around half an hour' Liam explained. 'This lets the paint charge using the solar rays from the sun and makes it glow brighter in the dark'.

Liam continued to speak of how he used PVA glue on the lid and covered it with glitter to make it look nice.

He said that he had seen these being made using glow sticks but realized that they would only glow for a certain amount of time. So he decided to use the glow in the dark fabric paint to see if it could be recharged in the sunlight! He had tested it a few times and found that it worked and that is how he came up with his idea!!

'Also' he said, 'I didn't have to spend my pocket money on a birthday present for my sister'.

Everyone in the audience laughed at this comment.

Liam jumped for joy to hear the Judges telling him they were so very impressed with his story and the way he had explained how he had worked everything out, that they had decided to give him first prize for his age group.

He was also invited to return next year to show his next invention.

'After all', the first judge said, 'science is about creating better ways to do things, as well as inventing completely new things'.

Later that same day Liam, John and Mary all took part in the interview for the Best Inventions magazine. They told how they had met the old man who had shared his story and that they wanted to share theirs with many more.

Liam felt like his life could not get any better - doing the thing he loved most, surrounded by the people who meant the most to him - but he knew that this was just the beginning for all of them to achieve their future dreams.

Dear Reader,

Thank you for reading our book.

We hope you found it informative
and enjoyable.

We would love to hear from you and hope
you will leave a comment either on our
Website https://lindahehirbooks.com/ or
on the websites it was purchased from
to let others know what your thought.

To make this easier we have added three
questions on the next page. Please feel free
to answer the questions and maybe your
mum or dad would be willing to add your
thoughts in the review section of Amazon,
Goodreads, Barnes & Noble, Facebook, etc.

Many thanks.

Question 1: What did you think about the story?

Question 2: What did you learn from the story?

Question 3: Do you think you will use what you have learned?

THE AUTHORS

Louise Blair is passionate about the provision of good customer service. Over many years Louise has provided customer service advice in a variety of settings. However, currently and for the last 9 years Louise works for a Social Research company undertaking interviews and reporting on a wide variety of research material. In conjunction with this she also runs her own direct sales business. It was through all that Louise has experienced that she learned the importance and need for continued self development. Louise's learning gave rise to some of the themes in the book ie: Believing in yourself; learning what you need to in order to succeed and believe you can do it.

Linda Hehir (RN, SCM, MScAcupuncture, AdCert in EFT) is and has always been passionate about health and wellness with her main career spanning over 40 years in NHS UK, as a nurse then as a quality/performance/nurse manager. In conjunction with her NHS career, Linda also works in Complementary Medicine as an EFT practitioner and as a qualified Traditional Chinese Medicine Acupuncturist and health coach. Upon retiring from the NHS Linda was keen to put her education and experience to good use. Believing in the 'Can Do' principle and taking a leap of faith and a broad base approach she published three books in different genres, which she believes all have an element of wellness to them. Her three books are this book developed for preteens, a self help guide for pain and a fictional adventure story inspired by a journey to Burma (Myanmar).